Samuel French Acting Edition

Summerland

by Arlitia Jones

SAMUELFRENCH.COM   SAMUELFRENCH.CO.UK

FOR PRODUCTION ENQUIRIES

UNITED STATES AND CANADA
Info@SamuelFrench.com
1-866-598-8449

UNITED KINGDOM AND EUROPE
Plays@SamuelFrench.co.uk
020-7255-4302

Each title is subject to availability from Samuel French, depending
upon country of performance. Please be aware that *SUMMERLAND* may
not be licensed by Samuel French in your territory. Professional and
amateur producers should contact the nearest Samuel French office or
licensing partner to verify availability.

MUSIC USE NOTE

IMPORTANT BILLING AND CREDIT REQUIREMENTS

SUMMERLAND had its world premiere at Cincinnati Playhouse in the Park in 2017. The production was directed by Michael Evan Haney, with lighting design by Kirk Bookman, scenic design by Paul Shortt, sound design/composer Matthew M. Nieslen, and costume design by Bill Black. The cast was as follows:

WILLIAM H. MUMLER . . . . Michael Rothhaar
JOSEPH TOOKER . . . . Billy Finn
MRS. MUMLER . . . . Whitney Maris Brown

SUMMERLAND was developed in the following workshop and staged reading:

Seattle Repertory Theatre, directed by Braden Abraham. The cast was as follows:

WILLIAM H. MUMLER . . . . Charles Leggett
JOSEPH TOOKER . . . . Darragh Kennan
MRS. MUMLER . . . . Cheyenne Casebier

Cincinnati Playhouse in the Park, directed by Michael Evan Haney. The cast was as follows:

WILLIAM H. MUMLER . . . . Barry Mulholland
JOSEPH TOOKER . . . . Ryan Wesley Gilreath
MRS. MUMLER . . . . Amy Warner

CHARACTERS

WILLIAM H. MUMLER – M, forty, large build, spirit photographer
JOSEPH TOOKER – M, thirty, slight build, investigator, one-armed
MRS. MUMLER – F, thirty-two – thirty-five, wife of Mumler, somnambulist

SETTING

Summerland takes place in New York City, circa 1869, in the upstairs photography studio of William H. Mumler, located at No. 630 Broadway.

ACT I

Scene One

(At rise, light of midmorning through skylight windows.)

(Inside the upper-story studio of spirit photographer **WILLIAM H. MUMLER,** *located at No. 630 Broadway in New York City, circa 1869.* **JOSEPH TOOKER** *stands facing* **WILLIAM MUMLER** *over a portrait chair with a posing stand positioned behind it.)*

TOOKER. This goes against nature.

MUMLER. This cures our nature, which is given to slouch.

TOOKER. Must I make any special preparations?

MUMLER. No.

> *(***TOOKER***'s growing agitation is contrasted with* **MUMLER***'s stillness.* **MUMLER** *remains mostly still when he is not required to perform some action in the scene.)*

TOOKER. Must you make any special preparations?

MUMLER. No.

TOOKER. I thought you would pull the curtains, dim the lights, at least.

MUMLER. Photography is the art of capturing light, not chasing it from the room.

TOOKER. Your procedure is ordinary?

MUMLER. You are expecting something *extraordinary?*

TOOKER. I'm not sure what to expect. I thought.

MUMLER. What?

TOOKER. Spooky. I thought it would be spooky. I think that's the word they use now.

MUMLER. On occasion I light a candle and chant while I roll my eyes back in a fit. I charge extra for those sessions.

TOOKER. That will not be necessary.

MUMLER. Thrift denies you a rousing chant. I am a good chanter.

TOOKER. Is this contraption completely necessary?

MUMLER. Yes.

TOOKER. Hard to imagine anything will occur in broad daylight. *(Beat.)* I'm trying to not be skeptical.

MUMLER. Mr. Wallingford, if you will take a seat and focus on that empty frame on the wall there.

TOOKER. Will something appear inside it?

MUMLER. No. The frame is for sale. Do you wish to purchase it?

TOOKER. I am happy there was room in your calendar for me to come in. Were you this busy when you worked in Boston?

MUMLER. Not so busy.

TOOKER. I confess my nerves are excited in this process. We are mucking about with something we don't fully understand.

MUMLER. There is nothing to be nervous about. I will be here with you the whole time. You have my word.

TOOKER. Is there no one else here to assist you?

MUMLER. I employ only myself. Do not be frightened.

TOOKER. I am not frightened. You come highly recommended.

MUMLER. My clients assure me it is a most pleasurable experience.

TOOKER. You've had some very famous clients, I understand. Our President Johnson, the esteemed Judge Edmonds, William Lloyd Garrison. Mrs. Lincoln has sat before your camera, has she not?

MUMLER. You know Mrs. Lincoln?

TOOKER. No. Not at all. People talk. I saw the photograph you made of her *(Beat.)* and her husband. You and your photographs are in all the newspapers. She provides you a worthy endorsement. It must have been a comforting surprise for her to see her husband in the print.

MUMLER. I do not discuss my clients or their results in their absence.

TOOKER. Of course. How long does this take?

MUMLER. Each portrait sitting spans the appropriate amount of time, depending on light conditions present in the studio.

TOOKER. Do I look dignified?

MUMLER. Decidedly.

TOOKER. Handsome?

MUMLER. I think so.

TOOKER. Tall?

MUMLER. I am not a magician.

TOOKER. You will be sure to get my good side. I don't want...

MUMLER. What?

TOOKER. I don't want my arm to show.

MUMLER. Your arm will not appear in the photograph because your arm is no longer attached to your shoulder.

TOOKER. Thank you for your reassurance.

> *(**MUMLER** approaches **TOOKER** with his hand out, and **TOOKER** mistakes this for an invitation to shake hands. He holds his hand out, but when **MUMLER** reaches him he puts his hand up to hold **TOOKER**'s chin, slowly rotating his head left to right as he tries to determine **TOOKER**'s good side. **TOOKER** lowers his hand.)*

MUMLER. As your photographer, Mr. Wallingford, the next question I must ask is which is your good side? Stern guardian of the law with a heavy gavel and a pitiless soul.

(Now he rotates **TOOKER**'s *chin to the right.)*

MUMLER. Or. Salacious fiend of the dark alleys with an opium habit and a fascination for criminal endeavor. Tell me, sir, are either of these your true occupation?

TOOKER. I am an honest man.

MUMLER. The camera will decide that.

TOOKER. Straightforward. I assure you.

MUMLER. Mr. Wallingford, you are a battleground. Two armies at war, one led by a righteous crusader, the other a black-hearted villain. In the middle is the photogenic Wallingford. Blended. Straightforward, as you wish.

TOOKER. Aren't you going to ask me, if I believe in this?

MUMLER. Believe in what?

TOOKER. In this. All of this. Spirits. Life after death. You. Your camera.

MUMLER. No.

TOOKER. Surely, that makes a difference?

MUMLER. Not to me. Not to the camera.

TOOKER. How is it done?

MUMLER. Harmony.

TOOKER. Harmony?

MUMLER. We must be in harmony with the spirits we ask to appear. You have someone in mind you would like to reunite with?

TOOKER. I would like to see my wife. She died a year ago. Do you think she will come?

MUMLER. You must let your longing for the one you lost fill your entire determination. If you have not already done so, please allow that to happen now.

(A moment.)

TOOKER. Mr. Mumler, do you believe?

MUMLER. In what?

TOOKER. Summerland.

MUMLER. I do.

TOOKER. But you don't know for certain.

MUMLER. I know there are distinct moments within the confines of this studio that I feel the warm breezes of its temperate climes. I smell the fragrance of its eternal blossoms.

TOOKER. You've seen Summerland?

MUMLER. No. Others have, but I have not. I cannot see the life-giving air surrounding me and yet my lungs pull it in. I have not seen Summerland, but I sense it there before me. I believe it is real. It is a matter of faith.

TOOKER. Can you make me believe?

MUMLER. Mr. Wallingford, all I can do is make you hold still.

TOOKER. This device is absolutely necessary?

MUMLER. It will bring clarity.

(**TOOKER** *sits in the portrait chair.* **MUMLER** *repositions the stand.*)

TOOKER. Maybe you don't have to push it so hard –

MUMLER. Mr. Wallingford, please, you must hold still.

TOOKER. Not one of my strong points.

(**MUMLER** *pushes* **TOOKER**'*s head onto the stand.*)

Agh! Sir! You are poking me!

MUMLER. Mr. Wallingford, hold still!

TOOKER. I'm trying.

MUMLER. I am helping you succeed.

TOOKER. How much longer? Are you ready to take the image yet?

(**MUMLER** *crosses to a table where a glass of liquid is preset. He drinks.*)

MUMLER. The plate has been ready since before you arrived. I myself have been prepared for the past five minutes. I been waiting for you to settle down.

TOOKER. Make the photograph.

MUMLER. Look at the frame on the wall.

TOOKER. I am looking.

MUMLER. Would you like to buy it?

TOOKER. No!

MUMLER. You will please tell Mrs. Mumler I did ask. She encourages me to be more entrepreneurial.

TOOKER. Can I blink?

MUMLER. Yes. The lens will not record an eyelid's movement.

TOOKER. If something appears, / should I look –

MUMLER. Quiet! Whatever happens, you will remain still.

TOOKER. What's going to happen?

MUMLER. Enough! We must concentrate.

> *(He removes the lens cap, then with great solemnity and ritual he places his hand on the camera and stands like this, absolutely still. Absolutely nothing appears to happen. As the portrait is progressing, a change comes over* **MUMLER**. *He is suddenly taken ill. He falters, keeping his hand on the camera.)*

(Weakly, to some unseen presence.) Edwin.

> *(***TOOKER** *remains in the chair, trying not to move.)*

TOOKER. Are you ill?

MUMLER. Quiet!

TOOKER. Is something there?

MUMLER. Be still!

> *(A moment passes.* **MUMLER** *rallies, replaces the cap, then falters again.)*

TOOKER. Is the photograph made?

MUMLER. Yes.

> *(***MUMLER** *falters.)*

TOOKER. Mumler!

(TOOKER crosses to MUMLER.)

MUMLER. *(Moan of discomfort.) (Quiet.)* Edwin.

TOOKER. What's wrong? May I be of assistance?

MUMLER. Help me.

> *(MUMLER reaches for TOOKER's prosthetic left hand, and TOOKER snatches it away from him, then shifts so MUMLER takes his right hand.)*

TOOKER. Come, Mr. Mumler. Stay here. I'll bring your wife.

MUMLER. No.

TOOKER. You are overcome.

MUMLER. Allow me a moment.

> *(As MUMLER sits he reaches and catches ahold of TOOKER's good hand. He presses it to his head and holds it there a moment.)*

TOOKER. You are ill. Your skin is warm.

MUMLER. Your longing for a spirit is very powerful. *(Beat.)* Your touch is kind.

> *(TOOKER jerks his hand away quickly.)*

I am sorry. After so much time among spirits, one forgets what it feels like to be touched by the living.

TOOKER. I should send for a doctor.

MUMLER. No! No doctor.

TOOKER. What happened?

MUMLER. I made your photograph.

TOOKER. Mr. Mumler, what ails you?

MUMLER. I am not sick. I am actually quite content at this moment.

TOOKER. Who is Edwin?

> *(TOOKER sees MUMLER is overcome.)*

Are you well?

MUMLER. …

TOOKER. Damn, man.

MUMLER. Spirits are here with us. There is something about you they esteem.

> (**MUMLER** *tries to take* **TOOKER**'*s prosthetic hand again, and* **TOOKER** *pulls back quickly.*)

TOOKER. Nothing special about me, I assure you.

MUMLER. Do not be afraid, please. They never want us to be afraid. Or alone.

TOOKER. I am not afraid.

MUMLER. I am never alone.

TOOKER. What happened?

MUMLER. What you came for – I made your photograph.

TOOKER. Was it successful?

MUMLER. The process is sound.

TOOKER. Did something appear?

MUMLER. I cannot say until I develop the plate.

TOOKER. But your reaction? This is all quite extraordinary.

MUMLER. No. This is quite ordinary.

TOOKER. Is this a frequent happening?

MUMLER. More than frequent. I feel the spirits' presence every time. Not always with this intensity.

TOOKER. Surely, you should see a doctor.

MUMLER. I am in perfect health. Quite returned to myself. You are safe.

TOOKER. You believe something happened?

MUMLER. Mr. Wallingford, we are surrounded. I feel them pressing their hands here, above my heart.

TOOKER. I didn't see anything.

MUMLER. The camera reveals what we cannot see – what is there beyond your physical senses.

TOOKER. Why didn't I feel anything? Why just you? If a spirit came because of me –

MUMLER. They come because of me. They are attracted to your longing, but I am the one who makes it possible for them to appear. I am the one they have chosen.

TOOKER. You are chosen? How do I know you are chosen when I see and feel nothing? That's my proof? Surely you provide more evidence than a fainting spell. If there is something here, because of me, because of my photograph being made, why can't I –

MUMLER. They have chosen me!

TOOKER. May I see the image?

MUMLER. Come back in three days. I will have your card printed.

TOOKER. Three days! Why three days –

MUMLER. We are done, Mr. Wallingford! Leave now! See Mrs. Mumler on your way out. She will make your return appointment.

(Silence.)

TOOKER. Do I give her my money?

MUMLER. Yes.

*(**MUMLER** makes to exit, presumably into his darkroom. **TOOKER** makes to follow him.)*

TOOKER. Mr. Mumler, if you'd allow me to observe the development process, I am very curious about how the entire –

MUMLER. Good day, Mr. Wallingford.

TOOKER. But. If I could just stand out of the way –

*(**MUMLER** exits, closing the door brusquely behind him.)*

(Lights change on the slam of the door.)

Scene Two

(Lights come up in a courtroom.)

(TOOKER is speaking before the judge.)

TOOKER. Yea, I have walked through the valley, Your Honor, where the War dead covered the ground, the blue and grey of Earth's lost armies. Death ravages without favorites. I suffered the stench of rotting corpses, searched in vain for a place to step my foot upon dirt not strewn with the maimed limb, crushed skull, or shattered rib cage of my fallen brethren. Not one of them rose up to walk beside me. Not one in a thousand. Not one in ten thousand. The dead remain resolutely dead. Am I to believe I saw no spirits for lack of a camera? Do not be taken in, Your Honor. William H. Mumler is a humbug. Do not fall for his talk of Eternal Summerland where our loved ones wait for us next to a bubbling stream surrounded by bright flowers and birds singing sweet melodies. Why are there birds in Eternity? Why birds? Are there also insects? Are there Raccoons? Do not be taken in.

(The sound of a gavel pounding a sound block.)

Your Honor, answering the mayor's request, I have just come from his studio. Under false name I paid to have him make my photograph with a spirit. I made out I wished to see my dead wife. It costs ten dollars to have your portrait made with a spirit. It also costs ten dollars to have your portrait made without a spirit, because sometimes the spirits miss their appointment. Mr. Mumler takes your money all the same. Or rather I should say Mrs. Mumler, takes your money. She guards the treasury and the door to the studio. Together, they are a well-matched team. They pander to our wounded selves. In three days I will return to receive my printed spirit photograph and at that point I will have the evidence to submit in a formal complaint against him. I played the gullible well and I doubt he will resist the temptation to place some woebegone woman in the frame with me. You see, I have no wife dead or living. I will catch him at his game and bring clear evidence against this fabulist and there will be a trial. The dead must stay dead. The living must keep their money.

(Lights change.)

Scene Three

(Lights up in the studio, three days later.)

*(**TOOKER** is entering through the door. **MUMLER**, who is organizing his glass plates, seems disturbed by **TOOKER***'s reappearance.)*

TOOKER. Mrs. Mumler sent me up. She said you were alone.

MUMLER. Mrs. Mumler knows I am never alone. Beware, if you trust a woman. Men marry for comfort. Women marry for something to do. Come in, Mr. Wallingford.

TOOKER. How are you feeling today?

MUMLER. Crowded.

TOOKER. Are you experiencing one of your spells?

MUMLER. My spells? I am not a mesmerist.

TOOKER. No. None of that *nonsense*. But you were taken ill, quite suddenly on my last visit here.

MUMLER. It is not illness.

TOOKER. I mentioned it to Mrs. Mumler just now and she dismissed it as nothing more than one of your "bouts of sympathy."

MUMLER. I will thank you not to discuss my physical state with my wife when I am not present.

TOOKER. I meant no disrespect.

MUMLER. Mrs. Mumler is not involved in the studio except to straighten and dust and point the way upstairs for my clients.

TOOKER. She does her own cleaning, Mrs. Mumler? You have hired no servants?

MUMLER. She keeps her household in her own fashion. I do not interfere with my wife's domestic sphere.

TOOKER. Does she see the images? Did she see my image? She gave me a rather mysterious smile just now. Leads me to believe there might –

MUMLER. She touches nothing without my direction. She is a dutiful wife.

TOOKER. She strikes me as a very zealous wife. Seems to me any man with such a wife as her does not have private moments.

MUMLER. You know the inner workings of others' marital arrangements and yet you yourself have never been married.

TOOKER. I have no spirit wife, you mean?

MUMLER. You have no wife at all.

(*A tense moment.*)

We are done with the pretense, are we not?

TOOKER. Yes, we are.

MUMLER. Wallingford is not your real name.

TOOKER. Tooker. Joseph Tooker.

MUMLER. Chief Marshal Joseph Tooker, to be exact. People talk. None of them leave off your title when they speak of you.

TOOKER. You've done your research.

MUMLER. Mrs. Mumler is a zealous wife and a competent researcher. You have a distinguished career in law enforcement. Bright future. Political ambitions, to be sure. Still there is something about you that is a false front. Your choice of a wooden limb, for instance. The sleeve rolled and pinned neatly to the shoulder socket would not be an effective look for a chief marshal, I imagine.

TOOKER. You are blunt.

MUMLER. You dissemble.

TOOKER. The mayor himself has sent me to find out your secret.

MUMLER. The mayor has his own secrets. If he wishes to make his public, alongside mine, that can be arranged.

TOOKER. Be careful.

MUMLER. I offer the same advice.

TOOKER. I have looked into your past.

MUMLER. What have you found?

TOOKER. History deems you trustworthy.

MUMLER. You pay me honor, sir.

TOOKER. However.

MUMLER. Ah.

TOOKER. The present is dubious.

MUMLER. What is my offense?

TOOKER. Fraud.

MUMLER. On whom?

TOOKER. You are swindling war widows and grieving mothers.

MUMLER. How so?

TOOKER. You deny death.

MUMLER. There is no law against that.

TOOKER. You earn far too much money doing it.

MUMLER. Is it the money or my victory over death that bothers you?

TOOKER. Let us focus on the money. You are putting God and his church out of business. Did you know nobody believes in Heaven anymore? Everyone's booking passage to Summerland. Local collection plates are scant of late. You are making the deacons jealous and the mayor nervous.

     (MUMLER laughs.)

TOOKER. You find it laughable?

MUMLER. I am but a humble spirit photographer. The fact that I am putting God and his church out of business affirms me. As for the mayor, he knows his own mother has had several successful sittings in front of my camera. I could call her as reference. If I have to.

TOOKER. You are a photographer with a special talent.

MUMLER. Again, you honor me.

TOOKER. Though there are some who say talent with the camera has nothing to do with it, that it is only your developing technique that makes you unique.

MUMLER. Shall I tell you what makes you unique? Chief Marshal Joseph Tooker.

TOOKER. I'm all ears.

MUMLER. And one arm. You are my first client ever who has returned to my studio after having a portrait made who has not immediately asked to see the results. I wonder that you are not at least curious about who is in your print.

TOOKER. You have already established there is no Mrs. Wallingford. I have no wife by any name.

MUMLER. It is not a woman.

TOOKER. I believe you to be a fraud.

MUMLER. You, a man pretending to be someone else, has seen through me. I am utterly transparent.

TOOKER. Hardly transparent.

MUMLER. You are calling me "solid," then? I blame Mrs. Mumler. The woman puts gravy on everything.

TOOKER. Mrs. Mumler, does she attend you when the spirits overtake you?

MUMLER. My "bouts of sympathy" are my own cross to bear.

TOOKER. Carrying the cross is an interesting allusion. Are you a Christian?

MUMLER. I attended church as a child. And you, Tooker? Christian? Would you call yourself a God-loving, care-giving, truth-telling man?

TOOKER. I can claim a couple of those qualities. I am washed in His blood, but long since strayed from His path. I am quite lost, and probably damned at this point in my life. How many people do you photograph, just the living, would you say?

MUMLER. I am fully booked most every day.

TOOKER. I wonder, if the spirits appreciate the woman's touch. Men's affairs always seem to run with more efficiency and style when a woman is in close proximity. She is always close by, is she not? Mrs. Mumler?

MUMLER. She is at her station.

TOOKER. This is your second marriage, correct? Her accent. She's not from Boston, is she? I'd say she's a bit farther south than Boylston. Closer to Virginia, I should think.

MUMLER. She was born in Virginia. Lost her entire family in the war. We met when she moved north soon after the surrender.

TOOKER. The spirits, do they wear a spirit timepiece?

MUMLER. There is no such device.

TOOKER. I wonder, how they know. When it's time for their sitting.

MUMLER. There was a young woman here earlier today. She also gave me a false name. It is a way of testing the process. Will the spirits show up without a proper name written in an appointment calendar?

TOOKER. Do they?

MUMLER. It was her eyes. The desolation in her eyes. Grief darkened her whole countenance. The spirits see a woman like this and they return to her bearing love. She came in, sat down, smoothed her skirt, and with a nod of her head indicated I should go to the camera. She lifted her hands from her lap, held them out in front of her, arms open as if receiving a gift. The Woman With Desolate Eyes cradled something with great affection. She tilted her head in a most tender aspect. I opened the camera. Sorrow receded and her face became radiant. If I have to pray to God in the Christian Church, or to the Indian spirit guides in Summerland, I will. I beseech whatever spirit she opened her arms to and looked for with such devotion to appear on her glass plate. O' God by any name, I pray earnestly, please, let that soul be in her portrait.

TOOKER. That was a compelling summons, I must say. But what if the Desolate Woman's arms remain empty?

MUMLER. She is welcome to try again.

TOOKER. And she will pay another ten dollars at that time?

(A moment of silence as the men regard each other.)

MUMLER. Chief Tooker, do you consider yourself a seeker of truth?

TOOKER. I am an honest man.

MUMLER. Yes. You said that last time you lied to me. The truth is right here. Do you wish to examine your print?

TOOKER. Enough of this. Air-up the swindle now, Mumler.

MUMLER. "You must let your longing for the one you lost fill your entire determination." You took my words to heart.

TOOKER. I will examine your equipment.

MUMLER. Not without a warrant.

TOOKER. I can take away your license to do business, if you do not cooperate.

*(With lightning speed, **MUMLER** reaches out to take hold of **TOOKER**'s fake arm. **TOOKER** is shocked into momentary stillness.)*

MUMLER. Tell me, does it still ache?

TOOKER. Let go.

MUMLER. This is no recent wound. Yet you still forget its absence. You reach out with it in your dreams. What is it you grasp for?

TOOKER. My dreams are private.

MUMLER. It still hurts.

TOOKER. Enough.

MUMLER. Does it burn? Do the fingers still reach to touch soft things?

TOOKER. Stop.

*(**MUMLER** releases **TOOKER**'s arm.)*

MUMLER. Do you know why that is? Your physical self has been separated from your spiritual self. In Summerland, you will be whole again.

TOOKER. You're telling me it will grow back.

MUMLER. It will not grow back, because in Summerland you never lost it in the first place. *(Beat.)* How did you lose it in this world?

> *(Beat.)*

TOOKER. The war.

MUMLER. The war. The war. Yes. The war. What of your photograph, Chief Marshal Tooker?

TOOKER. Damn the photograph.

MUMLER. You have carried your grief long enough. You must look and see who has returned to you. *(Beat.)* I assure you there is someone in the photograph with you.

TOOKER. I believe it to be a fraud.

MUMLER. Before you have even seen it?

> (**MUMLER** *produces his print and holds it out for* **TOOKER**. **TOOKER** *hesitates, crosses to* **MUMLER**, *takes the photograph, and examines the image.*)

You recognize the man standing next to you?

> (**TOOKER** *is shaken by what he sees.*)

TOOKER. *(Quietly.)* How?

MUMLER. His features are very distinct. Often, spirits appear only as vague outlines at best. You are fortunate.

> *(A moment passes.)*

Who is it?

TOOKER. How is it done?! What trick?

MUMLER. No trick. I can instruct you in the basic workings of the camera and plate, if you –

TOOKER. This is no normal photograph.

MUMLER. The photograph itself, is quite normal. As for the image on the plate, only you can speak to its enfabulated nature.

TOOKER. How is this possible?

MUMLER. Surely, that is the spirit you were longing to see. You called him back.

TOOKER. The image is false!

MUMLER. Do you wish me to make another photograph?

TOOKER. No!

(**TOOKER** *exits.*)

MUMLER. *(Yelling after him.)* I am willing to waive the ten dollars. If that is your concern.

(Lights change.)

Scene Four

(At the sound of the gavel, lights up in the courtroom.)

(MUMLER stands before a judge.)

MUMLER. I plead innocent, Your Honor. I stand before you wrongfully accused of fraudulent enterprise. In my own defense I claim no occupation beyond that as an honest spirit photographer. I alleviate grief. My process is sound and sincere. I invite you to my studio to observe. *(Beat.)* Your Honor, the real argument here is Spiritualism versus Materialism. We are debating the nature of man's spirit. Finite? Or non-finite? Judge Dowling, if you are a Materialist, and believe we are merely finite beings, then we have no further discourse and you must judge me a fraud surrounded by mere mortals who inevitably crumble into inconsequential dust and ash. All of our loved ones have become dust and ash. The land is covered in dust and ash. It pains me to think of Mrs. Mumler cleaning my studio last week. Her polishing rag brought shine to every smooth surface and metallic fitting. If, in the end, man becomes nothing more than finite particles of dust and ash sifting onto the furniture, I wonder whose lost sweetheart did she set cartwheeling into the afternoon breeze along Broadway when she leaned out the window to shake her dust rag? *(Pause.)* I am a Spiritualist, I follow the teachings of Reverend Andrew Jackson Davis who compels us to push back the veil between this world and the next where our loved ones wait for us in the paradise of Summerland. Your Honor, if you are a Spiritualist like me, then it is our belief that the spirit of man, my spirit, your spirit, every spirit in this room is an infinite being that exists beyond utility of flesh and bone. It is our belief that the spirit of man is eternal, incorporate and free to communicate with the living, according to the spirit's own will. It is our belief we can once more look upon the departed wife we never stopped loving, or the cherished face of the lost child we long to hold. If Summerland is where your belief leads, or at the very least your curiosity, then we have much to converse upon. The oldest and deepest mystery: What happens to us in the end? Where do we go when we die?

(Lights change.)

Scene Five

(Lights up in the studio as **TOOKER** *is preparing to investigate* **MUMLER**'s *process.)*

TOOKER. How do we begin?

MUMLER. Focusing the camera.

TOOKER. May I?

MUMLER. Certainly. Go under the hood. Use the knobs on the right. Bring the chair into focus. You will see the image upside down.

TOOKER. It's done.

*(***MUMLER*** proceeds to the next step: the glass plate.)*

I would examine that plate.

MUMLER. There must be no fingerprints.

TOOKER. I will be vigilant.

MUMLER. The chemical solution will stain your skin. I have a pair of gloves. You will need one glove. Please, put it on.

*(***MUMLER*** produces a pair of gloves and hands one glove to* **TOOKER**.*)*

Do you need my assistance?

TOOKER. No.

*(***TOOKER*** puts on the glove.)*

*(***MUMLER*** holds up the glass plate.)*

MUMLER. *(Showing* **TOOKER**.*)* The glass plate.

TOOKER. Clear and unclouded, no engraving?

MUMLER. It is imperative the glass remain unadulterated.

TOOKER. May I hold it?

MUMLER. Please hold it by the edges.

*(***MUMLER*** hands* **TOOKER** *the glass plate.* **TOOKER** *holds it up to examine it in the light.)*

TOOKER. Pristine. A man can see all the way to God through this, if he bothered to look.

(MUMLER looks through the glass.)

MUMLER. I can only see to the crown molding.

TOOKER. You are a humbug.

MUMLER. If you have only come to look for a humbug, I predict that is all you are going to find.

TOOKER. I am here to find the truth.

MUMLER. Then you must observe with an impartial eye.

TOOKER. An impartial eye? According to my portrait sitting last week, I don't have one. What was it, this one is the judge and this one is the criminal? Or do I have them backwards?

MUMLER. They are transposable. You have that kind of face. We will now retreat to the darkroom.

> *(Lighting changes to a red glow to indicate the men are now in the darkroom.)*

> *(MUMLER takes the plate back from TOOKER.)*

TOOKER. Proceed with the first step. I confess I am eager to observe. And participate.

MUMLER. Observe. Onto the plate we spread the collodion solution.

> *(MUMLER spreads solution on the plate while TOOKER watches.)*

TOOKER. Fascinating.

MUMLER. Hold your exuberance. I would not have you exhaust yourself when we have so many steps to complete.

TOOKER. Why the red light?

MUMLER. Spooky. I learned that word from you.

TOOKER. It is a good word.

MUMLER. I like it.

TOOKER. Are there spirits in your darkroom?

MUMLER. There are spirits in every nook and cranny of this studio. We must never forget we are surrounded. They are right here beside us.

TOOKER. You honestly believe such bunkum?

MUMLER. Yes. My belief is in everything I do. Every thought, every hope guides me to Summerland. My loved ones are there waiting for me. I take much comfort in that.

> (**MUMLER** *holds up the plate with solution on it.*)

Satisfied?

TOOKER. Proceed.

MUMLER. Next, while the plate is still wet, it must be dipped in the silvering box.

> (**MUMLER** *produces a silvering box that the glass plate can be inserted into.*)

> (**MUMLER** *inserts the glass plate into the silvering box.*)

The silver catches light. It adheres to the collodion and makes it photo-reactive. We must wipe the plate clean on the back. You will assist me.

> (**MUMLER** *pulls the plate out of the silvering box.*)

TOOKER. Happily.

> (**TOOKER** *assists* **MUMLER** *by wiping the back of the plate with a chamois while* **MUMLER** *holds it.*)

MUMLER. You must think of the camera's lens as an invitation. The photographer's job is to open the invitation to the world and bid welcome to whatever truth lies in its field of vision.

TOOKER. That is how you call the spirits before your camera?

MUMLER. I have told you, they come of their own will.

TOOKER. And the living pay the fee.

MUMLER. Summerland has no currency recognized by my tailor or my landlord.

TOOKER. Ten dollars. Have you considered that's an exorbitant fee? When I was a soldier that would have been almost a month's wages.

MUMLER. A spirit photograph is an object of great value. Spirits do not favor the throng. The price is fixed to exclude skeptics and the vulgar multitude.

TOOKER. In other words the poor have no spirits who wish to visit them.

(**MUMLER** *hands the prepared plate to* **TOOKER,** *who holds it carefully around the edges.*)

MUMLER. Now the plate is placed in the light-proof holder. This is how we expose it.

(**MUMLER** *demonstrates opening the holder screen.*)

If you will.

(**MUMLER** *holds the plate holder out to* **TOOKER** *so he can place the glass plate.*)

This holder fits into the camera.

TOOKER. May I see it?

(**MUMLER** *shows the open plate holder to* **TOOKER,** *demonstrating how it works.*)

MUMLER. The light-proof holder is as important as the camera itself. One ray of unwanted illumination and the entire process is compromised.

(**MUMLER** *holds the light-proof holder to* **TOOKER,** *who places the prepared glass plate into it.* **MUMLER** *then closes the holder and hands it to* **TOOKER.**)

TOOKER. It is complex, this process.

MUMLER. Two antagonizing forces, a war of light versus dark, an interdependency of friend and foe.

TOOKER. You speak like a soldier.

MUMLER. The war entered all our lives.

TOOKER. Spiritualists were said to make the best fighters. Bravery unsurpassed. They had no fear of death. You might have made a great warrior.

MUMLER. I would have made a great coward. I do not fear death itself, but I do fear dying and I do respect bullets. They poke holes in your body that should not be there.

> *(Beat.* **MUMLER** *takes the light-proof holder back from* **TOOKER**.*)*

Once the plate is secure we take it to the camera.

> *(The lights change again to return the men to the regular studio light.)*

> *(***TOOKER** *takes a moment to adjust his eyes to the change in light.* **MUMLER** *is unaffected, due to familiar practice.)*

TOOKER. I must let my eyes adjust. What are you doing? I must see.

MUMLER. We prepare for the exposure. The holder is inserted into the camera.

> *(***MUMLER** *starts to place the holder into the camera.* **TOOKER** *stops him.)*

TOOKER. May I?

MUMLER. Certainly. Slide it into the camera, this way, and open the holder.

> *(***MUMLER** *hands the plate to* **TOOKER**, *who places it in the camera.* **MUMLER** *drinks a preset tonic.)*

TOOKER. It's done. Now what?

MUMLER. Exposure.

TOOKER. You will open the invitation?

MUMLER. Yes. You will please take a seat.

TOOKER. I will not.

MUMLER. In order to make a portrait, I need a subject.

TOOKER. Not me.

MUMLER. Who, then?

TOOKER. Mrs. Mumler, surely her fair visage could be of –

MUMLER. She does not care to have her photograph made.

TOOKER. You can't make your wife hold still, is that it? Why can't you just make the photograph with no one in the chair and wait for Benjamin Franklin or George Washington? Maybe Thomas Jefferson? No shortage of dead presidents.

MUMLER. Sit in the chair.

TOOKER. Mumler, you sit in the chair.

MUMLER. I am the photographer.

TOOKER. I am the chief marshal. You have set up the camera. We have adjusted the focus. I will place your neck in the stand this time and you will instruct me in how to make the photograph from this chair. I assure you, I will follow every instruction to the letter.

MUMLER. This is an unorthodox method.

TOOKER. But effective for investigative purposes.

MUMLER. Surely, you are the better subject –

TOOKER. I will never sit before your camera again.

MUMLER. Who was he? The man in your photograph?

TOOKER. I do not wish to speak on him.

MUMLER. Someone you knew? It was clear you recognized him.

TOOKER. Leave it.

MUMLER. I re-examined the plate. He appeared to be standing / over you looking down at –

TOOKER. I will not speak of it! Sit down.

> (**MUMLER** *takes a seat on the portrait chair, and* **TOOKER** *starts to position the posing stand.*)

MUMLER. You will capture my good side. I wish to appear favorably.

TOOKER. I will capture you as you are.

> (**TOOKER** *pokes* **MUMLER** *with the stand this time, and* **MUMLER** *gives a little yelp of pain.*)

MUMLER. Chief Tooker, you are wrong about death.

TOOKER. My opinion on death is that it is inevitable and final. I am not wrong.

MUMLER. You stated before that I deny death. I do not. It is grief I deny. Surely you do not object to that?

TOOKER. Grief is unavoidable. Grief makes us human.

MUMLER. Grief makes us broken. It robs our souls, leaves us with a gaping wound where once there was light. Spiritualists heal these wounds. The space beside us right here, there is somebody here.

TOOKER. Nobody is beside me.

MUMLER. Allow it to happen. There is always somebody here. Somebody here. Right here. Right here. *(Whisper.)* I can feel him. Here.

TOOKER. Who do you feel?

MUMLER. Edwin. Smiling child. Eight years old. Died of influenza. His mother followed him soon after. The boy was an exceptional child. Edwin Wallace Mumler. My son. I had just taught him to play chess. The current Mrs. Mumler and I do not have children. Will not have children. He was everything to me. When he died I did not want to go on living. How could I be without him? The Mumler name ends here. With me. The hope of my mortal family died with him.

TOOKER. I am sorry.

MUMLER. I want him back.

TOOKER. Impossible.

MUMLER. Right here! He is standing right here. I've seen him. The first time he appeared I was making a test portrait much like we are doing today. I positioned the camera. I opened the lens. Took my seat. I felt. Strange. Light-headed. Fevered. Visited upon. Edwin was very much on my mind. I perceived I was no longer inside the room, rather I was transported inside my own mind. Lost inside my emotion and longing.

TOOKER. You have an over-excited imagination. I don't believe any of it.

MUMLER. You don't realize how little that matters against what I know to be true. I passed out in front of the open camera. That camera. Long enough for the plate to be properly exposed. Gradually, I returned to my wits, the feeling had lessened enough that I was able to rise and close the camera, I was so affected. I took to my sickbed. Later, I developed the plate. I saw him. He was there. Edwin was in the image. My son standing beside me. He had been there the whole time. He is on the plate and the print. I will show you.

TOOKER. I cannot hold that as proof.

MUMLER. Proof? That is all you are here to find? You must have proof before you accept Summerland to be true?

TOOKER. I am not here to prove Summerland is true. I am here to prove you are a fraud.

MUMLER. You may investigate every movement, every moment of my practice, Chief Marshal Joseph Tooker, but you will never disprove the joy and love I felt when I saw Edwin's face form on the plate. Grief has no hold. Surely, you can see the work I do provides healing comfort in a world where young men are marched off to war and infants die in their mothers' arms. The grief of this land would be too much to bear.

TOOKER. Let us see, if Edwin appears.

MUMLER. The spirits are here. Go to the camera.

(TOOKER *goes to the camera.*)

TOOKER. I expose the plate now?

MUMLER. Carefully. Do not disturb the camera.

TOOKER. Are you going to swoon?

MUMLER. It will hurt. There is always pain when grief flees the body. I am ready. Make the exposure.

(TOOKER *exposes the plate. The two men remain absolutely still for a moment while the photo is being made.*)

*(Gradually, a change comes over **MUMLER**, though he is still trying to remain still. He is in great discomfort.)*

TOOKER. You're hurting, already? Should I stop? Or should I wait for the chanting to begin?

*(Suddenly, a thundering, loud, violent knocking is heard in the studio. **TOOKER** startles.)*

What is this?

(The knocking sound is heard now in a different location of the studio.)

Was over there. Now, here.

(Silence.)

Is this a new trick? Is Mrs. Mumler performing her offices as poltergeist?

(Loud raps heard from the floor and immediately after that from the ceiling.)

Who's there? Enough of this ghost racket. Surely, it's been an appropriate length of time.

*(**TOOKER** decides the photograph has gone on long enough. He covers the lens and turns his back to **MUMLER** as he removes the holder. While he is preoccupied with this, **MUMLER** lets out a gasp and sinks from the chair to the floor in great discomfort. **TOOKER**, holder in hand, turns to see **MUMLER** on the floor.)*

Come on, Mumler. The show is over. Mumler!

*(**TOOKER** moves to **MUMLER**'s side. **MUMLER** is passed out.)*

Are you ill? Can you speak? Stop this, Mumler! Enough! There are no spirits here!

*(The door to the studio opens as if by its own locomotion. **MRS. MUMLER** steps into the threshold. She is dressed in black and has a wrathful look on her face. She fixes **TOOKER** with a baleful stare.*

She enters the room in a trance-like state. The door slams behind her.)

He's taken ill. Help me. He was fine, talking to me. I was making his photograph.

*(When he realizes that she is not responding to him, **TOOKER** stands to face her, the plate still in his hand. He cringes when he looks in her face and backs away. She follows him swiftly and locks eyes with him until he is still.)*

(A clicking is heard, spidery and skeletal, clacking, crackling, fast and slow, it builds.)

(Sniffing the air, overwhelmed by an aroma from the past.)

Lilac. I smell lilac.

*(The tapping and clicking again. **TOOKER** sniffs at the room.)*

Where is it coming from?

(One loud bang.)

*(**MRS. MUMLER** moves very close to him.)*

(Softly at first, the sound of clicking and tapping is heard. Like the sound of one knitting needle tapping against a solid object. Then another small tapping is heard. Then another.)

(The tappings grow in intensity and number, different rhythms and cadences, all around the room until it sounds as if a thousand knitting needles are tapping everywhere at once. The sound grows louder and deafening, like a crashing rainfall, a deluge of sound. Then, abruptly, it stops and a crushing silence is left.)

MRS. MUMLER. Get out.

*(The door flies open. **TOOKER** exits. **MRS. MUMLER** surveys the room for a moment. She regards her husband, then takes a heavy black*

background cloth and covers him up. She stands in the center of the room. Soft tapping resumes as she raises her arms high on each side, palms up. When her hands reach her head height she slowly turns them over and lowers them back to her side.)

(As her hands come down the lights dim and taps subside, following her motion. The world fades to darkness.)

(Blackout.)

(Intermission.)

ACT II

Scene One

(Lights up on the studio, three days later.)

(Stillness. The room appears empty at first, but **MUMLER** *is there, standing or sitting, conscious, totally covered head-to-toe in the heavy black background cloth.* **MRS. MUMLER** *enters from the main studio entrance wearing all black, carrying a tray with a glass of liquid. She acknowledges his presence to herself, in the manner of a wife who is no longer charmed by her husband's eccentricities.)*

(She crosses and stands next to him. She lifts the glass from the tray. A moment passes, then **MUMLER***'s open hand emerges from under the cloth and waits to receive something. She places the glass in his hand, which disappears under the cloth again.)*

(Another moment passes while she waits.)

*(***MUMLER***'s hand appears again with the empty glass. We hear the front doorbell ring.)*

*(***MRS. MUMLER** *hears the bell but makes no move to answer it. She exits through a back servants' entrance.)*

(The bell rings again.)

(The bell rings a third and final time, and we hear knocking from the street.)

*(***MUMLER** *does not budge.)*

(This scene is continuous with the next.)

Scene Two

(**TOOKER** *appears in the doorway of the studio moments later. He crosses to* **MUMLER** *and pulls the heavy cloth to the floor, revealing* **MUMLER** *underneath.*)

MUMLER. I knew it was you.

TOOKER. You are a psychic now?

MUMLER. You are becoming predictable.

TOOKER. Your wife wasn't downstairs. I had to conduct my own self up. She's close, though?

MUMLER. She is away.

TOOKER. Away, is she? How far away?

MUMLER. We are alone for now, Tooker.

TOOKER. You could find a better hiding place.

MUMLER. I was not hiding. I was attempting to be alone.

TOOKER. A difficult task for someone who lives at the threshold of Summerland. All the coming and going. Dead and living –

MUMLER. What do you want?

TOOKER. I have a court order.

MUMLER. A Materialist victory.

TOOKER. Judge Dowling has authorized me to collect evidence.

MUMLER. Forensics will not save you.

TOOKER. I am protected by the truth.

MUMLER. What is the truth?

TOOKER. In my case the truth is what I can see and hear, prove with my own senses. In your case truth is a wire attached to Mrs. Mumler's wrist. She's a talented performer, I'll give her that.

MUMLER. Leave my wife out of this.

TOOKER. I don't think I can. What I am trying to figure out is who is protecting whom. Mrs. Mumler, how is she connected to all of this?

MUMLER. She is responsible for arranging my calendar and is content performing her household duties.

TOOKER. Many words describe your wife. Content is not one of them. She has her own proclivity for the spirit world.

MUMLER. I am the one they have chosen.

TOOKER. You are the one who is famous. Your wife stays in the background.

MUMLER. She prefers it that way. Her life is here and she is private.

TOOKER. She is still familiar in the offices of the Sanitation Committee. Did you know? She has no qualms about picking through a dead soldier's effects. Your helpmeet is renowned for her dedication. Some like her. Many do not.

MUMLER. Her work with the Sanitation Committee allowed her to bring solace to grieving families whose loved ones were lost in the war. She believes we should not rest until all the bodies return home and regain their names. We owe them that. Are you investigating me or my wife?

TOOKER. If there's something you'd like to share about her background, it might reflect favorably on your own case.

MUMLER. There is no wrongdoing in my wife's past. She is a devoted Spiritualist.

TOOKER. You've both overreached. Had you confined your vocation to the common class, no one would've noticed. Ah, but I forget, the spirits do not care for the vulgar multitude.

MUMLER. This is America. Surely, I am free to socialize among whichever class I choose. All men are equal in democracy. The terrible war proved that, did it not? It has had a profound effect on all of us. If we are born equal, it follows then we die equal. An entire generation died equal in that war. You see why a man of my calling should be so popular. I have more work than I have years to live, I am afraid. I should get back to it –

TOOKER. Yes, I can see how profoundly the war has affected you. The glass plate we made together, I had it developed.

MUMLER. How did it come out?

TOOKER. Fraudulent.

MUMLER. Well, that was only your first try. You will get better.

TOOKER. Do you know who appears in the frame with you?

(A moment of expectation builds.)

MUMLER. *(Beat.)* Is it Edwin?

TOOKER. You really don't know?

MUMLER. How could I? You have the plate.

TOOKER. Edwin is a humbug. You made him up. Admit it.

MUMLER. How dare you!

TOOKER. Abraham Lincoln! How dare you!

> *(***TOOKER*** *takes a printed photograph out of his jacket and throws it at* ***MUMLER.****)*

> *(***MUMLER*** *is stunned and very confused. He was not expecting that.)*

Does he have another appointment today? I wonder, if I knock, will he knock back?

> *(***TOOKER*** *knocks loudly on something to make his point.)*

President Lincoln, are you here? Hello, sir? Good Ol' Honest Abe. Look at the photograph! Oh, he likes having his photograph made. Especially by you, it seems. Since you've become so familiar, maybe you can tell me, why is he in a different light than you? He's wearing the same suit as before in the photo with Mrs. Lincoln. He has no change of clothes in Summerland?

MUMLER. You are mocking our slain president.

TOOKER. I am mocking you, Mumler, don't be so thickheaded. Abraham Lincoln. You bring shame upon yourself with this trick. Look upon your lie.

He comes to you in a photograph and smiles like a proud father upon a worthy son. I've seen that elephant before and I won't buy it.

> (**MUMLER** *stares at the photograph. He is still trying to collect himself.*)

MUMLER. I am honored to have him beside me –

TOOKER. The audacity of you. You prey upon the sorrow of a torn nation and the grief of his widow. You disgrace his memory. If I were to make your photograph right now, would he show? Perhaps he's attending a séance across town, using his spirit fingers to pluck the strings of a floating banjo. Or could it simply be that it's not possible for him to come because Mrs. Mumler has vacated the shadows for the time being? Even spiders leave their cracks to go wandering the wide ceiling.

MUMLER. You insult my wife.

TOOKER. She will survive, believe me. Tell me, where is the black guller? Is she somewhere behind the wallboard cracking her toes?

MUMLER. You go too far!

TOOKER. I've hardly begun! I am calling out your lies. Stand down, Mumler. (*Taking a paper out of his pocket.*)

> (**TOOKER** *hands him the court order.* **MUMLER** *reads it.*)

MUMLER. You are not taking my camera.

TOOKER. I have the authority.

MUMLER. You do not have the strength.

TOOKER. Are you threatening me?

MUMLER. I would not fight a one-armed man.

TOOKER. One arm or two, I am a formidable opponent.

MUMLER. I have done nothing wrong.

TOOKER. You have a photograph of Abraham Lincoln. Where is it? Let me see it. You have your choice. Confess it to me right now, or to the judge later.

MUMLER. I have nothing to confess. I have done nothing wrong.

TOOKER. Did you pay for the image? Let's acknowledge the corn before you embarrass yourself. Where is your library? How many images have you bought to use on your unsuspecting marks? I will examine every one of your plates, if I must.

MUMLER. This warrant does not include my plates.

TOOKER. The judge will grant me an order to remove them, as well.

MUMLER. You defame me. For that I can forgive you. But you would disrespect the spirits and despoil the very bridge I have forged to Summerland.

TOOKER. Happily.

MUMLER. I have done nothing wrong. I have told you my motives. I absolve us of grief. What about the photograph I made of you, Tooker? I do not know who the man standing beside you is, but you do. The sight of him is enough to make you turn cruel. Do not rob me of my life's work. The plates are fragile. Please, they are all I have.

TOOKER. I am taking your camera. That is all for now.

MUMLER. How will you do it? You only have one arm.

TOOKER. I will kick it down the stairs and out onto the street, if I have to. This camera is coming with me. Stand back, or I will arrest you.

> (**TOOKER** *starts to deal roughly with the camera.* **MUMLER** *panics.*)

MUMLER. No! You will damage it. Let me do it.

TOOKER. All right then, help me.

MUMLER. I will carry it for you. Please.

TOOKER. Your cooperation will be noted.

(TOOKER stands back and allows MUMLER to gather his equipment. He is careful and reverent with the camera.)

MUMLER. You are confiscating my life.

TOOKER. I am dismantling your lie. Go.

(TOOKER opens the studio door. The two men exit, MUMLER carrying the camera.)

(Lights change.)

Scene Three

(Much later that same night, the studio in candlelight. The main entry door is ajar.)

(MRS. MUMLER stands motionless in the center of the studio, as if in a trance. She is wearing a voluminous outer robe. A quiet moment passes. Suddenly, she startles violently to wakefulness with a gasp or small scream, breathing heavily and disoriented as if she has just received a great shock.)

(Another moment passes while she regains her composure.)

(She takes off her robe and drapes it on a chair. She continues taking off articles of clothing, whatever they are, until she is standing barefoot and clothed only in a simple linen shift. She then raises her arms from her sides, palms up, and holds them in the air, forming a cross with her body.)

(Another moment.)

MRS. MUMLER. Chief Marshal Tooker, you will enter. Unless you prefer to conduct your investigation through the door frame.

(The door creaks open all the way and a chagrined TOOKER enters the doorway.)

TOOKER. Madam, I am sorry. I did not mean to spy.

MRS. MUMLER. Oh, Chief Tooker, but you did mean to spy. Otherwise, I would not have disrobed for you. See? No wires.

TOOKER. You are playing a dangerous game. Does your husband know you sent for me?

MRS. MUMLER. No game. And no, he doesn't know.

TOOKER. What if I tell him?

MRS. MUMLER. You won't. You're here hoping I'll turn against him.

TOOKER. Will you?

MRS. MUMLER. We must be truthful with one another. I hide nothing from you other than what modesty decrees, my mortal body inside this linen shell. I am part of my husband's investigation, am I not? You would like to examine me, would you not?

TOOKER. I would speak with you.

MRS. MUMLER. So. We are talking.

TOOKER. Put your hands down.

MRS. MUMLER. Close the door.

> (**TOOKER** *hesitates. She lowers her hands.*)

TOOKER. Where is your husband?

MRS. MUMLER. Indisposed. He has taken to his sickbed since the confiscation of his photography equipment. You have unmanned him. He is alone. Dejected. Utterly abandoned.

TOOKER. Perhaps you should go to him.

MRS. MUMLER. Oh, I don't think so. It's never my company he desires. The spirits are his only friends. They have not come to him since you stole his camera.

> (**TOOKER** *closes the door.*)

TOOKER. I did not steal his camera. I had a court order to remove his equipment for inspection. I intend to prove he is a fraud in court so I can shut down this shameless ghost factory you're running here.

MRS. MUMLER. "Ghost factory." *(Laughs.)* My husband did not tell me you were such a comic.

TOOKER. I am not here to make you laugh. I am in earnest.

MRS. MUMLER. Earnest. One should always be earnest, if one lives as a pessimist.

TOOKER. I think of myself as a Positivist.

MRS. MUMLER. Positivist. Materialist. Jurist. Please, if we are going to use labels, I prefer Joseph and Katherine.

TOOKER. You are too familiar.

MRS. MUMLER. If only that were the worst thing you've said about me.

TOOKER. Forgive me.

MRS. MUMLER. I do.

TOOKER. What part do you play in this scheme?

MRS. MUMLER. Ah. We're getting to it. How I earn my keep? Joseph, sit with me.

> (**TOOKER** *hesitates when she indicates a bench or somewhere in the studio where they can sit in close proximity.*)

I won't bite. Or pick your pockets, if that's what you fear.

TOOKER. I am not afraid.

MRS. MUMLER. Why do you hesitate?

TOOKER. Your manner is very much changed since the last time I saw you.

MRS. MUMLER. Is it? I don't remember being any way but as I am now.

TOOKER. You are a somnambulist.

MRS. MUMLER. Am I? How exciting! You've given me another label. Now, come sit.

> (*She motions him to sit. He sits.*)

Do you trust me?

TOOKER. Not at all.

MRS. MUMLER. Wisejay. You would make such a good husband.

TOOKER. You are married already.

MRS. MUMLER. Yes. I am aware.

TOOKER. The prosecutor is trying to make his case for fraud against your husband. Are you ready to declare a new allegiance?

MRS. MUMLER. What, if I am?

TOOKER. You will escape scrutiny.

MRS. MUMLER. My husband is on trial. Not me.

TOOKER. Your cooperation may discourage me from opening a separate case against you after your husband has gone to jail.

MRS. MUMLER. A case against me? On what grounds? Is it a crime for a wife to perform her household duties?

(*A moment passes while she considers her situation. The soft knocking is heard.*)

TOOKER. Are the sound effects part of your household duties? You are a complete fraud.

(*The knocking stops.*)

You don't have much of an accent anymore, but I can still hear something below Mason-Dixon. Virginia, if I'm not mistaken.

MRS. MUMLER. You are mistaken.

TOOKER. Your husband already told me you were born there.

MRS. MUMLER. Did he? How forthright of him.

TOOKER. You haven't been back to Virginia since the war, because you can't go back, can you?

MRS. MUMLER. There's nothing for me in Virginia. My life is here now.

TOOKER. Yes, it is. A brand new life as the second Mrs. Mumler. But I'm curious about the old life before you changed your name.

MRS. MUMLER. A woman is required to change her name when she marries.

TOOKER. In the offices of the United States Federal Army there is a file with the name Delores Katherine Cartier on it.

MRS. MUMLER. Is there?

TOOKER. Fascinating woman. No family. No past. She came into existence during the war. She is suspected of being a double agent. Despised by both sides. She was a resourceful medium in Richmond. Ingenious cover, she passed military secrets in the form of spirit messages.

MRS. MUMLER. The dead have no stake in who wins a war.

TOOKER. But her enemy contacts did and they were very much among the living. Troop movements, the distribution of certain vital supplies, her spirits were very liberal with information. Too liberal.

MRS. MUMLER. Why did you never arrest such a woman?

TOOKER. We lacked the means to identify her. She has never been photographed.

MRS. MUMLER. She must have been a modest woman.

TOOKER. I doubt it. Have you ever allowed your husband to make your photograph?

MRS. MUMLER. The camera does not favor me.

TOOKER. Hopefully you will fare better with the engraver's art. Your likeness will be published in the press, alongside your husband's when you testify. I'm betting there are some who will recognize you. For who you are. Or who you were. *(Beat.)* Do we have an understanding?

MRS. MUMLER. You're good at this. You must already see yourself as a politician.

TOOKER. I am a lawman.

MRS. MUMLER. For now. Joseph, sit with me, please.

TOOKER. Yes or no? What is your answer?

MRS. MUMLER. Please, sit.

TOOKER. What is your angle?

MRS. MUMLER. Dialogue. That's all. You're a nervous rabbit.

TOOKER. You are a scary hawk.

MRS. MUMLER. Such flattery. Here, take hold of my wings.

(She reaches out to take his hands and he pulls away, embarrassed by his prosthetic.)

TOOKER. Madam, no.

MRS. MUMLER. Katherine, please. Do not be embarrassed. Joseph, will you look at me? Keep your eyes open. Look into my eyes. Don't look away. Here is my open hand. I place it in your good hand. We touch. Hold fast to each other, like so. Feel my hand. My palm against yours.

Our fingers entwined. We touch. Here is my other hand. Open and reaching for your absent hand. Hold fast. Feel my hand in your absent hand. My palm and your palm. Fingers entwined. We touch. Like so. You can feel my hands. Both my hands.

TOOKER. Yes.

> *(They stare directly at each other. A long moment passes.)*
>
> *(Softly, the question knocking is heard, then stops.)*

MRS. MUMLER. Someone would speak with you.

TOOKER. What do you want?

MRS. MUMLER. Not me.

TOOKER. Who is it?

> *(A soft, continuous knocking reply is heard.)*

MRS. MUMLER. A woman.

TOOKER. How can you tell?

MRS. MUMLER. Lilacs. You smell them?

TOOKER. *(Quietly.)* Yes.

> *(The soft knocking stops.)*
>
> *(**TOOKER**'s state seems to have grown very relaxed and vulnerable.)*

MRS. MUMLER. Joseph, I want you to take three deep breaths. Breathe in the lilacs.

> *(A moment passes. **TOOKER** breathes.)*
>
> *(More continuous knocking is heard.)*

You remember lilacs from your childhood?

TOOKER. My mother loved them. She planted them along our fence.

MRS. MUMLER. Breathe in your mother's lilacs.

> *(He breathes. A moment.)*

You remember springtime as a child?

TOOKER. Yes.

MRS. MUMLER. She told you to stay inside the fence.

TOOKER. I got in trouble when I left.

MRS. MUMLER. Where did you go?

TOOKER. I heard the music. I followed. I wanted to see the man in the tent.

MRS. MUMLER. Smoke. Lights. The man is on a stage.

TOOKER. He's holding something.

MRS. MUMLER. What is it? Can you see it?

TOOKER. A dog.

MRS. MUMLER. A little brown dog.

TOOKER. Wagging his tail.

MRS. MUMLER. You like the dog.

TOOKER. He's whining.

MRS. MUMLER. You're worried about the dog.

TOOKER. He's going to kill it.

MRS. MUMLER. How is he going to kill it?

TOOKER. With a sword.

MRS. MUMLER. Why is he going to kill the dog?

TOOKER. So he can bring it back to life.

MRS. MUMLER. What is the man doing?

TOOKER. He's putting the dog in a canvas bag, pulling the drawstring around its neck. I can see the dog's face. He looks scared. He doesn't like him.

MRS. MUMLER. Why doesn't he like the man?

TOOKER. The man is raising the sword. The sword is in the air.

MRS. MUMLER. What happens next?

TOOKER. No!

> (*Suddenly,* **TOOKER** *explodes from his seat to get away from her as fast as he can. The knocking stops abruptly.*)

MRS. MUMLER. Joseph!

TOOKER. Stand back! Stay away from me.

> (*They stand apart, regarding each other.* **TOOKER** *trying to regain his composure.*)

MRS. MUMLER. Remain calm. You are in a vulnerable state.

TOOKER. Do not come near me.

MRS. MUMLER. Do not move away.

> *(She makes physical contact for a brief moment.* **TOOKER** *breaks it.)*

TOOKER. Madam, put your clothes on!

MRS. MUMLER. *(Small laugh.)* Oh, Joseph. I should have explained before we started. I only do exactly as I see fit.

TOOKER. I pity your husband.

MRS. MUMLER. So do I. Who was the man in your photograph?

TOOKER. Is that why I'm here? You're hoping I'll tell you who it is?

MRS. MUMLER. I'll find out, one way or another.

TOOKER. If your husband is found guilty of fraud, he will go to jail. I'll see to it you follow him.

MRS. MUMLER. My husband is not a fraud. He is chosen. Ask him. He'll tell you, "I am chosen."

TOOKER. Yes. We've had that conversation. If you are found guilty, you will hang for treason.

MRS. MUMLER. Is that a threat?

TOOKER. How did you know about the tent?

MRS. MUMLER. Lawilda told me.

TOOKER. My mother is passed on.

MRS. MUMLER. I know. She's delighted we've finally met. Now she can communicate with you whenever she likes. She knows we have so much in common. We have both survived a war.

TOOKER. Easy to do when one is willing to switch sides.

MRS. MUMLER. Easy to do when one side is right and the other wrong.

TOOKER. You are motivated by the just cause? You really expect me to believe that?

MRS. MUMLER. War is at its best when you're backing the winner.

(Knocking is heard, then stops.)

Someone in Summerland is looking for you.

(Soft knocking is heard again, then stops.)

I think the spirits led you here for a reason.

TOOKER. Judge Dowling sent me here. I am not a gudgeon. Do not treat me like one of your marks. I warn you.

MRS. MUMLER. Now I am confused. I assumed you enjoyed my treatment of you just now. It's the dilation of the pupils. Involuntary response to pleasure. Poor Joseph, the Positivist, betrayed by your own physiology.

TOOKER. I made a photograph of your husband. Why did Lincoln appear in it?

MRS. MUMLER. My husband worships the man.

TOOKER. You don't share the sentiment?

MRS. MUMLER. I could take him or leave him. I'm not sure he deserves a single blade of Summerland grass, but I am in the minority. Oh, he's probably listening. I should say something nice about him.

TOOKER. Did you put Lincoln's image on your husband's plate?

(Soft knocking is heard, then stops.)

MRS. MUMLER. I hear he was a good joke-teller.

TOOKER. What about the plate of Mrs. Lincoln with the president? Did you forge that as well? Did someone in the War Office give you the negative?

MRS. MUMLER. How many legs does a dog have, if you call the tail a leg? You should like this, it's about a dog. Come on, guess.

TOOKER. Does your husband share the profits with you?

MRS. MUMLER. Four. Calling the tail a leg doesn't make it a leg. Isn't that a corker?

TOOKER. Did you forge the Lincoln plate?

MRS. MUMLER. How do I know you didn't put the image of Lincoln on my husband's plate?

(The soft knocking starts again.)

TOOKER. Are you trying to implicate me now?

MRS. MUMLER. For one of us to be innocent, we must all be innocent.

TOOKER. You're a rare one, if you think you can convince anyone of that.

(The knocking stops.)

Why has the knocking subsided? Are you out of apples to drop?

(A studio table jumps into the air and crashes down with a bang.)

MRS. MUMLER. That was a very large apple.

TOOKER. You are a clever spider.

(Continuous knocking is heard.)

How are you doing that?

MRS. MUMLER. I am doing nothing. Examine me. Look for the wires. Hidden instruments. Apples.

TOOKER. You are using a code word. Where is your accomplice? Hidden in the cupboard? Packed beneath the floorboards?

(TOOKER stomps the floorboards. After he does, the continuous knocking stops abruptly, and then the same number of corresponding knocks is heard.)

MRS. MUMLER. They like you.

(She holds up her hand for him to see and taps her thumb and forefinger together three times in a noiseless gesture. The knocks come three times, significantly louder than TOOKER's.)

They like me better. Oh, what a story they tell, Joseph. It's a wonder you can even look at a dog now.

TOOKER. You are a practitioner of toe-ology.

MRS. MUMLER. You think I make that noise with my feet?

TOOKER. Mediums are ill-jointed devils.

MRS. MUMLER. You find me ill-formed?

> *(She lifts the hem of her shift far higher than is necessary to reveal her toes.)*

TOOKER. No.

> *(The question knocking is heard, then stops.)*

MRS. MUMLER. Oh, they are persistent. You're going to have to answer them. Who was the man in your photograph?

TOOKER. A fraud, nothing more.

MRS. MUMLER. You are covering something. Joseph, you know the dead are not as good at keeping secrets as the living. I will find his name. Disguising nothing as an arm doesn't make it an arm. Disguising guilt as an ache, doesn't make you less guilty. The man with the dog, what was his name?

TOOKER. He was a deceiver.

MRS. MUMLER. What was the deceiver's name?

TOOKER. Magnifico. The Giver of Life.

MRS. MUMLER. "The Giver of Life." What a title! God himself is not so arrogant. He killed the dog in front of you and promised to bring it back to life. But it didn't happen that way.

TOOKER. No.

> *(The knocking is heard, continuous.)*

MRS. MUMLER. He beheaded it and placed the head and body in a box. And then he asked the audience...

TOOKER. He asked us, if we wanted him to bring the dog back to life.

MRS. MUMLER. And you stood up in the front row shouting.

TOOKER. I begged him to bring the dog back.

MRS. MUMLER. He said yes. "I have the power to give life." Then he closed his eyes and waved his hands.

> *(The knocking grows a little louder.)*

TOOKER. He opened the box.

MRS. MUMLER. And what did you see?

TOOKER. You tell me.

(*The knocking is a little louder and more complex.*)

MRS. MUMLER. He opened it and there was the dog.

(*The knocking stops.*)

Alive and wagging his tail. Perfectly fine.

TOOKER. I was ecstatic.

(*Beat. Silence for a moment.*)

MRS. MUMLER. When did you figure out it was a twin?

TOOKER. After the show. I went behind the tent and saw the bloody head laying in the straw where his assistant had emptied the box.

MRS. MUMLER. You fell down on your knees. You cried. Until that moment you had believed the dead could come back to life.

TOOKER. I was a child.

MRS. MUMLER. A child who had just learned one day you yourself would die.

TOOKER. I'll expose you as a fake before that happens.

MRS. MUMLER. Magnifico was a fake. The man standing with you in the photograph, he is real. Do we have an understanding?

(*Lights change.*)

Scene Four

(Lights change and **TOOKER** *is gone. It's dusk the next evening.)*

*(*MUMLER *is sitting alone in his chair. He is holding a glass plate in his hand.* **MRS. MUMLER** *enters. She's wearing her robe and shift. She's carrying a tray with a glass on it.)*

MRS. MUMLER. You have been sequestered here for hours. Working on anything interesting?

MUMLER. I practice the art of solitude. It is my attempt to engender peace. I have sat still in this chair in the span of time it takes the sun to travel from that pane of glass to this pane of glass and have produced nothing by the passage of its light.

MRS. MUMLER. The sun is almost set, you great silly mountain of a husband.

MUMLER. Where have you been?

MRS. MUMLER. Mountain, move thyself out of that chair to a more temperate latitude. Come closer to me. *(Holds up a drinking glass.)* I promise it will lighten your countenance.

MUMLER. *(Dangerous.)* I prefer my current location.

MRS. MUMLER. What plate is this?

MUMLER. Leave it.

MRS. MUMLER. Secrets? How mysterious. Let me see.

MUMLER. I said leave it!

(He grabs her wrist, causing her to wince, then pushes her away.)

You touch nothing unless I tell you. Understand?

MRS. MUMLER. I would never. I give you my word.

(He lets go of her.)

Your tonic, husband.

(She hands him his tonic and he drinks half of it.)

MUMLER. The plates are mine. They are my work. My life's work. Now he is threatening to take them. I will be left with nothing.

MRS. MUMLER. Do not mope, William.

MUMLER. I have no purpose in life.

MRS. MUMLER. Oh, not true. You are the one they have chosen.

MUMLER. I have no camera.

MRS. MUMLER. A temporary setback. The spirits will not abandon you for the lack of apparatus.

MUMLER. The spirits have no reason to come. I have no lens to open for them.

MRS. MUMLER. Then buy a new camera, you lumpy old hill. Really, William, I would have thought you could work that out for yourself. Bad publicity brings flies same as good, though we might have to use a bit more honey.

MUMLER. The press is dragging my name through the mire. They have accused me publicly and ruined my reputation.

MRS. MUMLER. You invited the attention. Did I not warn you the press would turn on you? If you had listened to me –

MUMLER. I will not be scolded by a wife. Especially one who does not see fit to dress herself. You are common. Tooker claims you are strung with wires.

MRS. MUMLER. Why don't you check for yourself? Search me.

> *(She tries to get him to touch her body. He pulls away in disgust.)*

MUMLER. Leave me be! You forget yourself.

MRS. MUMLER. I am exactly as I was when you married me.

MUMLER. If the judge rules me a fraud, I am sunk. We are sunk.

MRS. MUMLER. You are not a fraud.

MUMLER. You don't know what it's like for me. I answer their call, and for that I am disparaged.

MRS. MUMLER. You are not the only one to be condemned. I have read all sorts of foul epithets attached to my name. According to the *Times*, you are married to a spider, an ugly beast of malice. It hurts my feelings. I am a foul harridan and there is nothing to be done about it.

MUMLER. Don't play the victim. We are both in a fester of your own making.

MRS. MUMLER. My making? What have I ever done but stand beside you from the start?

MUMLER. Mary Todd Lincoln. How could you lead her up the stairs without knowing who she was?

MRS. MUMLER. She had a veil over her face. Black spectre of arrogance, she was.

MUMLER. How dare you speak of her that way.

MRS. MUMLER. She is the one to blame.

MUMLER. You weren't paying attention. If I had known it was her, I would have had Judge Edmonds ask her for her discretion. Foolish woman was announcing to the whole world she'd had a portrait made with her husband before I had even developed the plate.

MRS. MUMLER. None of that matters. Her husband appeared. You are a powerful spiritualist. No one else has come close to your success.

MUMLER. Abraham Lincoln –

MRS. MUMLER. Comes to you because of your gift.

MUMLER. He is in my photograph, now. Why?

MRS. MUMLER. He honors you. How grateful he must be. You provide the agency for him to return to a world that sorely misses his leadership. Your ability is growing. Stronger every day. You feel it, don't you?

MUMLER. You are ambitious.

MRS. MUMLER. If I am ambitious, it is only a reflection of your power. Everything I do is in support of you and the spirits who come to you.

MUMLER. Did you somehow tamper with the glass?

(**MRS. MUMLER** *is stunned a moment by the accusation.*)

MRS. MUMLER. What are you saying?

MUMLER. Tooker is asking me about your past. Why?

MRS. MUMLER. He's only casting about, desperate to make a case against you.

MUMLER. Perhaps he is making a case against you.

MRS. MUMLER. Against me? He's the one who removed the plate and left you lying on the floor unconscious. How do we know he didn't tamper with the glass? How do we know he's not trying to frame you?

MUMLER. You are putting the blame on a chief marshal?

MRS. MUMLER. He seeks your glory. What a coup it would be for him to bring down the famous William Mumler, the country's most renowned spirit photographer. It would be his name in all the papers, then. Tooker is good at lying, he's already proven that.

MUMLER. If he were here, he would tell me you are lying.

MRS. MUMLER. Has he turned you against me?

MUMLER. If it is true, you dishonor everything I do.

MRS. MUMLER. Oh, woe! I am wounded to the heart! Cast me out! Throw stones at my head! Pierce my breast with poisoned barbs but do not accuse me unjustly for something I did not do.

MUMLER. Your performance is growing stale.

MRS. MUMLER. O' poor disappointed husband! O' mountain of useless scorn! Stand thou before me and judge! Meanwhile the water is rising beneath your feet. If you are not careful, you will find yourself with nowhere to stand, you stupid moon-faced fainting goat!

(In a flash movement **MUMLER** *catches her by the throat with one hand. He is not strangling or hurting her, nevertheless she is immediately still. Their eyes are locked. A moment passes.)*

MRS. MUMLER. *(Frightened.)* William. You and I are in this together.

MUMLER. You are alone. Not a single soul, living or dead that longs to be reunited with you. What does that feel like?

(His grip tightens.)

MRS. MUMLER. Please.

(Soft knocking is heard.)

The spirits are here. If you send me to Summerland, what will I tell little Edwin?

(He tightens his grip.)

MUMLER. Edwin! Are you here?

MRS. MUMLER. *(Quietly.)* William! I swear the child himself is watching through the veil. He sees you. Do you feel his fear?

MUMLER. Edwin? Would you show yourself? I have no camera. He is here and I have no camera.

(The knocking stops.)

MRS. MUMLER. He's gone.

MUMLER. Did you tamper with the plate?

MRS. MUMLER. No.

*(***MUMLER*** searches his wife's face, holds eye contact for a moment.)*

MUMLER. You are not afraid of me.

*(***MRS. MUMLER***'s manner grows stoic. He lets go of her.)*

You have no idea the pain this causes me.

*(***MUMLER*** sits. She retrieves the tonic glass.)*

MRS. MUMLER. I'm sure I could not bear it.

MUMLER. You will speak to the judge tomorrow. You will dress yourself modestly, and testify that I am chosen by the spirits. He may yet confirm I am innocent.

(She hands him the tonic.)

MRS. MUMLER. We already know you are innocent. *(Referring to his tonic.)* Now finish up.

(MRS. MUMLER picks up the plate MUMLER made of TOOKER in their first meeting.)

Interesting man, our Chief Marshal Tooker.

(She looks at the plate.)

Even more interesting is the man standing beside him. A soldier, Union Army, judging by his uniform. So much sorrow in his face. He is drawn to Tooker.

(MUMLER stares at the tonic glass in his hand. He grows sleepy.)

MUMLER. Do you know who…?

MRS. MUMLER. Shh. No worry. The spirits will not abandon you in your hour of need. The truth will out. Water flows underground, I can hear it, even if I can't see it yet. Sweet dreams, dark mountain. Close your eyes and feel the clouds gather at your crown.

(MUMLER is asleep in his chair. MRS. MUMLER takes the glass plate from his hand and exits, leaving MUMLER asleep, snoring for a moment.)

(Lights change.)

Scene Five

(Lights come up in the courtroom.)

*(**MRS. MUMLER** addresses the judge. **TOOKER** will eventually appear in the background.)*

MRS. MUMLER. There is no way we could've had any foreknowledge of who she was, Your Honor. She wore a black veil over her face, poor dear angelic woman. She arrived in a rented carriage, with no insignia I recognized, quite anonymous. I'm sure if you ask her yourself, she will confirm her appointment had been made by another party under the name of Mrs. Lindall. She said not a word to me in the front hall but immediately ascended to the studio, her tread heavy, so burdened with sorrow. My husband said he'd never seen such a face. Grief had ruined her. Those were the words he used. She remained with him the better part of an hour, I remember. When she descended her step was lighter, as if some piece of brilliance had taken refuge in her breast. She was veiled once more, but I could tell she moved with a lingering reverence for her encounter. Our hearts brimmed with compassion and tenderness. When my husband developed her plate we saw who appeared on the glass beside her, we knew instantly and only then that President and Mrs. Lincoln had come to the studio. We are reverent. The great man who saved our Union from being torn asunder now appears with my husband on a plate he made with the assistance of Mr. Tooker. It is a great honor. My husband serves the Lincolns proudly –

TOOKER. It is a great swindle. / Do not be fooled by this woman.

(The sound of a gavel drowns him out, calling the court back to order.)

MRS. MUMLER. As I was saying, I in turn serve my husband in whatever small capacity I am able as his wife. Yes, Your Honor, I do make all arrangements in my husband's appointment calendar. Of course, many clients come to us under the guise of a false name. It's a way to test if the spirits are real. Testing them is one thing. To deny them when they show, is quite another. When spirits have taken all the trouble to come from Summerland to pose, the least we can do is reattach them to their names, lest their identities become like lost appendages cluttering the fields of eternity. That is death done twice to them, if we lose their names. I always learn the names of the spirits that come before my husband's camera. All the names, Your Honor. I find them.

   (Lights change.)

Scene Six

(Lights up on **MUMLER** *and* **TOOKER** *in the studio.)*

(The two men stand facing each other over the camera, which is returned to its position. The door is ajar.)

TOOKER. It's over. There is your camera returned.

MUMLER. You have brought my life back to me, scrutinized, measured, its inner workings tested. The exposed heart forced back in and sealed up. And now you return it to me. Desecrated. Did you find what you were looking for?

TOOKER. The Judge saw no evidence of fraud.

MUMLER. Have you found what you were looking for?

TOOKER. I found nothing inside your camera.

MUMLER. It is just a camera. There is nothing to be found there.

TOOKER. Judge Dowling has ruled you are not guilty.

MUMLER. Not guilty is not the same as innocent, is it? What about you Chief Tooker? What is your judgment?

TOOKER. My judgment no longer counts. The investigation is over.

MUMLER. Every man counts. You should remember that from the war. Do you believe in my innocence?

TOOKER. Not for a second.

MUMLER. Who was he? The man in your photograph?

*(***MRS. MUMLER** *has appeared in the servants' entrance.)*

MRS. MUMLER. Answer him. Surely my husband deserves an answer after everything you have put him through. Go ahead. Say his name.

TOOKER. The case is concluded.

MUMLER. The judge has found me not guilty. Chief Tooker returns my equipment. Hard feelings shall be put away.

MRS. MUMLER. We are long past hard feelings, William. Chief Tooker asked me to turn against you. He offered me absolution. Tempting. But what would I tell him? You are a boring old mountain. I would have to make up something just to keep his interest.

TOOKER. Your husband's investigation is over. Yours is just beginning. You, we will prove guilty.

MUMLER. Guilty? Of what?

TOOKER. You really don't know her deceit?

MUMLER. What fraud are you accusing her of?

TOOKER. Not fraud, we've moved on to treason. Spiders move in the dark where it is hard to discern the color blue from the color gray. During the war your wife traded in military secrets for her living.

MUMLER. It was not uncommon for many women to serve the cause.

TOOKER. Which cause are you talking about, Mumler? She served both North and South with an agile will. If your wife ever served a single cause, it was only ever her own.

MUMLER. *(To* MRS. MUMLER.*)* Are the allegations true?

MRS. MUMLER. He's only worried about his own record. Chief Marshal Tooker cannot abide defeat so now he comes after me. Where is your evidence?

TOOKER. You sound scared, Mrs. Mumler.

MUMLER. She can play a broad range of emotions. She's quite believable at scared.

MRS. MUMLER. You would know, you make me play it enough.

TOOKER. I will arrest you for treason, Mrs. Mumler. How many lives were lost because of your meddling? Did you know your wife worked as a medium during the war? She conducted spirit circles in Richmond where she passed information to both sides. A double agent, a black heart with no allegiance or faith to either cause, is despicable. The séance was an effective cover. Mumler, I imagine you saw a business partner in her before you ever saw a wife.

MUMLER. I believed the spirits guided us together.

TOOKER. Matchmakers in Summerland, are there? By rights, she should have been a medium of great renown, except that she had to change her name and disappear to avoid a military tribunal. And then there's the convenient lack of any photograph of her, which is rich considering she married you. But the press has now printed her engraved image alongside yours. You will be recognized.

MRS. MUMLER. Charles Bailer.

*(At the sound of his name, **TOOKER** is greatly affected, as if he's punched in the gut.)*

That was his name. Charles Bailer. He died at Gettysburg.

TOOKER. His death is a matter of record. I know you have been to the Sanitation Committee. You have found my requests to locate his body. I made them on behalf of his mother.

MRS. MUMLER. Charles Bailer died at Gettysburg, and you did not. They say once a soldier is gravely wounded something goes out of him forever. What did you lose? Charles Bailer knows. It was more than your arm. Tell my husband what he did that day. Tell him. Or I will.

TOOKER. He saved my life.

MRS. MUMLER. But not your arm.

TOOKER. Did you receive a spirit message for this revelation or did you just look at me to know that?

MRS. MUMLER. Charles Bailer was shot six times.

TOOKER. They shot him once. He died instantly.

MRS. MUMLER. No. He was shot six times.

TOOKER. You have misread my report.

MRS. MUMLER. You didn't put that in your report, did you?

TOOKER. My account is accurate.

(Clicking sound starts, continuous.)

MRS. MUMLER. There is a copse of trees a few yards away.

TOOKER. He fell. I was trying to drag him –

MRS. MUMLER. No! No, you aren't. He's dragging you. He's pulling you toward the trees. You can't move. You *won't* move.

TOOKER. He fell beside me.

MRS. MUMLER. He's lying on top of you.

TOOKER. He took a single round in the back. He died immediately –

MRS. MUMLER. No, he is still alive. His body is covering yours.

TOOKER. How dare you!

MRS. MUMLER. He's shot again, in the ribs. And again.

TOOKER. He was dead already.

MRS. MUMLER. He lingers. He is alive. He suffers.

TOOKER. He died when they shot him.

MRS. MUMLER. He endures. He feels his life blood ebbing away. He's crying. He's bleeding. So much blood.

TOOKER. He was dead.

MRS. MUMLER. He's crying. He's begging for mercy. He's cursing your name.

TOOKER. He gave his life! There was nothing I could do!

MRS. MUMLER. You're pushing him onto his side. Using him as a shield.

TOOKER. I couldn't move.

MRS. MUMLER. He blames you.

TOOKER. I couldn't move!

(Clicking stops.)

MRS. MUMLER. You wouldn't move. Charles Bailer is a heavy burden.

TOOKER. Charles Bailer gave his life for honor. Something you know nothing about.

MRS. MUMLER. His body has disappeared. Now the only remains of Charles Bailer are on the photograph that you would deny.

TOOKER. How did you do it! How did you get Charles Bailer in the frame?

MUMLER. Spirits come of their own will. They come out of love.

MRS. MUMLER. Charles Bailer will speak for himself. Chief Tooker, I am standing between two worlds. I have a message for you. Would you hear it?

TOOKER. No. No more of your lies. You are a traitor.

MRS. MUMLER. I have his image. I have his name. I have the story. Heartbreaking story. One that would sell well in newspapers. Charles Bailer would be the new sympathetic hero of Summerland. And you, Chief Tooker, would fall to the ranks of dishonor and shame.

TOOKER. I will bring you to justice!

MRS. MUMLER. You are not here for justice, Joseph. You were never here for justice. You came for your ambition. You came because you are afraid of dying. Afraid of reckoning. The Giver of Life has actually aced the trick this time. The dead have returned and you stand before them in your guilt, stripped of your lie. Charles Bailer sees you clearly for what you are. If you could hear, what I hear. If you could unstop your ears to their lament and anger. The dead. The dead. So many dead! Eternity is bloated with our dead! There is no rest in peace for our armies of dead. We rob them of it. The spirits are forced to return to us because we won't let them go. We are drowning in the waters of their despair and you have convinced yourself it's love. I have let you believe it. Love sells better than indictment.

MUMLER. You would destroy everything I do.

MRS. MUMLER. What do you do, William?

MUMLER. I help people to heal. I lighten their grief.

MRS. MUMLER. You take their ten dollars. Nothing more.

MUMLER. False woman! They come to me.

MRS. MUMLER. You have no connection. There is not a soul in this world or the next who longs to be with you. You are alone. How does that feel?

(A moment passes.)

MUMLER. Edwin.

MRS. MUMLER. He is not here. He has never been here.

MUMLER. You lie! I can feel him!

MRS. MUMLER. You feel what I allow you to feel. It's not Edwin. It was never Edwin.

MUMLER. Please, Edwin.

MRS. MUMLER. Your son is dead. His death was his escape, and you know it.

*(A moment passes. **MUMLER**'s world is shattered.)*

They do not come because of you. You are a man in a room with a camera. You are not chosen.

TOOKER. I want the plate of me and Charles Bailer. Mumler!

MRS. MUMLER. You will never erase Charles Bailer.

TOOKER. I will see you hang.

MRS. MUMLER. Not before I see you disgraced. I have the plate. I have the name. I have his story. Chief Tooker, you have no courage for this fight. Charles Bailer will not save you this time.

*(**MRS. MUMLER** exits through the open studio door.)*

(Lights change.)

Scene Seven

(Lights up on the entire studio.)

(The stage is empty. From all around we hear a great shattering of glass, crashing and breaking. **MUMLER** *is destroying his entire body of work with the exception of one last plate. When the crashing stops he appears, carrying his last plate in one hand, a hammer in the other. He drops the hammer and stares at the plate a moment, then presses it to his heart. He remains like this a moment, emotionally and physically exhausted.)*

(Lights dim.)

Scene Eight

(Lights up on the studio, weeks later.)

*(***TOOKER*** is in the studio, in mid-conversation.)*

TOOKER. He tied something around it to stop the bleeding. They shot him in the back. He fell on top of me. Still alive. He couldn't move anymore. I did not move. I would not move. I was consumed with terror beyond anything I've ever known. His face was pressed in my hair. He cursed me. Damned me to the devil. I felt the next round hit his body. Shots all around us. I pushed him onto his side and I held on, pressed myself against him. Hiding. His body between me and the enemy. The last thing Charles Bailer knew in this world is that I am a coward. They shot him four more times. He lived through the first three.

(A moment.)

I am alive because of him. He is dead because of me. His remains vanished. The Sanitation Committee has still found no trace. His mother still writes asking me to keep looking.

MUMLER. Did you tell her about the photograph?

TOOKER. No.

MUMLER. Will you?

TOOKER. I would give anything in this world, if the photograph of myself and Charles Bailer had never been made. If she did tamper with the glass, I don't know where your wife would've found his image. His mother has assured me she knows of no photograph ever taken of him during his life.

MUMLER. And yet, he is there on the plate. Undeniable.

TOOKER. I will tell his mother about the photograph, eventually. And I will tell her he died in my arms.

MUMLER. I don't think anyone would fault you for –

TOOKER. I didn't tell you all that so you could absolve me of my past. Or my grief.

MUMLER. Why did you tell me?

TOOKER. It's the truth. I owed you that.

MUMLER. You owe me nothing.

TOOKER. I put you out of business.

MUMLER. No, you did not. I quit of my own accord.

TOOKER. I heard you were leaving town.

MUMLER. Yes. I am back to Boston, next week.

TOOKER. You'll start over.

MUMLER. No.

TOOKER. It will take a little time for this to blow over. Your customers will come back. Business will pick up.

MUMLER. It is not my customers who left. The spirits have abandoned me. I am quite alone in my studio.

(Silence.)

TOOKER. Any word of her?

MUMLER. No. She is vanished.

TOOKER. I will keep looking for her.

MUMLER. I will try to forget her.

TOOKER. *(Beat.)* One thought I keep having.

MUMLER. What is that?

TOOKER. My mother. She really did love lilacs. In the springtime she placed bowls of blossoms in every room of our house.

MUMLER. Everyone's spirit mother loves lilacs.

TOOKER. Really?

MUMLER. If not lilacs, roses then. Two flowers men can actually recognize and know the names of.

TOOKER. I can also recognize tulips.

MUMLER. They have no smell.

TOOKER. I'll be damned.

(A moment passes.)

What of Edwin?

MUMLER. Edwin. I have not seen my son since the first time, the only time he came to me. *(Pause.)* I was a stern father. That I cannot absolve.

TOOKER. Tell me the truth, did she plant him?

MUMLER. I had not even met her yet. Edwin came to me. It was just me. I was alone when I made that photograph. My son was standing beside me. I swear on his name.

TOOKER. How?

MUMLER. All I can offer is my belief.

TOOKER. This brings me no comfort. If it's true, if the dead can return...

MUMLER. Perhaps in time you will welcome the idea.

TOOKER. Mumler, you are right. We are never alone. Charles Bailer stands beside me every day. Right here. I must live with that.

MUMLER. Yes.

TOOKER. Perhaps this isn't goodbye, then. Perhaps the next time I see you it will be in Summerland.

MUMLER. Perhaps.

TOOKER. We should make a pact to meet up somewhere. There is a stream in Summerland?

MUMLER. Yes, there is a stream.

TOOKER. Then I will see you on the banks. Are there fish?

MUMLER. Enormous fish.

TOOKER. That settles it. We will spend eternity catching fish. I hope there are worms.

MUMLER. If we are dead, there is no shortage of worms.

TOOKER. That is comforting.

MUMLER. Would you like me to make your photograph? My rates are quite affordable these days. I will capture your good side, position you so your arm does not show. Please.

(A soft tapping is heard that builds to a brief crescendo of knocking. Then soft knocks in a slow

rhythm. The two men stare at each other across the portrait chair.)

(Lights down to natural light coming in the windows, then out to black. Tapping sounds in the dark.)

End of Play